WOLF ON THE HIGH SEA

IDLEWYLD MATES
BOOK THREE

RENEE HEWETT

Way out in a little suburb of Denver sat one of Esme Baer's favorite bakeries.

It was one of those places you missed if you weren't looking for it, nestled in the middle of downtown. Not that just a few blocks of businesses made much of a *downtown*. The bakery melted into its surroundings, and unless you were in the know, you would assume it was an insurance brokerage. Yet, on closer inspection, the single-story standalone red-brick building was special. The front consisted of large picture windows with white-wash trim and a black awning over the bright, friendly yellow door.

Esme's stomach rumbled in anticipation at the mere sight of Pastry Pack.

The inside was just as friendly and delicious-smelling as you could hope. Sugar, vanilla, peanut butter, and more delicious scents wafted over to Esme. Since the bakers' equipment took up most of the small space, the front customer area was tiny, consisting of a glass display, checkout counter, and a few small tables

Esme, bakery connoisseur that she was, and supporter of shifters in general, had been a patron of the Pastry Pack since opening day. The two wolves built their dream into a successful and popular business.

Of course, the men gained experience and confidence each year the business ran, which meant even yummier and unique concoctions. This was an added bonus in Esme's book. They had a special gimmick where they came out with two limited-time-only cookies every week. *Get them now, before they're gone forever!*

Forever didn't actually happen. People demanded certain ones come back. Esme happened to know that if you were in the right position—as she was—you could have your choice of cookies catered for special events.

"Ms. Wilder!" Thatcher called out to her the moment she walked through the door. "What a surprise to see you!"

The younger of the brothers was clean-shaven, tall, with lean muscles, though he had the same dark hair and eyes, and charming smile that his brother had.

Brett and Thatcher Cowans didn't look the type you'd expect to own and run a bakery, though they did. They created all the recipes and menu ideas themselves and baked everything with their own two hands. The brothers were wolf shifters, alpha personalities at that, but they stuck to themselves rather than lead packs.

They grew up that way—loners and bakers. Over the years, she learned that their parents traveled a lot for work, often leaving their sons alone. Left to their own devices, the boys cooked whatever they wanted. For kids, this meant baked goods for dinner.

They didn't open a bakery right away, though. It was a second career for both brothers. Thatcher had originally gone to law school. Brett, poor wolf, was a lost soul for the early part of his young adulthood. Esme assumed that opening the bakery with his brother had probably saved his life in more ways than one.

"I'm just returning from some business in Idlewyld," Esme explained, walking to the display to see what they had available that day. "And you know I can't be so close to Pastry Pack without stopping in. I love to see what you're baking up."

"Idlewyld isn't exactly close," Thatcher teased, already pulling out a plate and piling treats on it for her.

"Close enough. Colorado is Colorado, and a few

hours drive is worth it for your mouth-watering treats." Esme looked behind Thatcher. "Is your brother here?"

"Brett, get out here," Thatcher called toward the back. "Special customer."

The older brother lumbered out from the back. He was a few inches shorter than Thatcher but broader, with more pronounced muscles covered in tattoos. When Brett's eyes locked on Esme, his face brightened up into a smile just as friendly as his little brother's.

"Ms. Wilder, great to see you! Here for the cookies, I assume?"

"Great cookies and even better company," Esme beamed back.

"Take a seat, Esme. I'll warm these up for you."

"What?" Brett balked at his brother. "I've got a batch coming out of the oven. Hang tight." He hurried away and quickly returned with a tray loaded down with fragrant freshly baked cookies.

As she waited, she couldn't tell which bit of anticipation bubbling inside her was more potent—the one for the warm gooey delicious cookies or the one for starting her next matchmaking scheme.

Esme took a moment to savor her treats. The peanut butter chocolate chip cookie melted on her tongue. These boys had a real gift, now it was *her* turn to share her own gift. "Do you boys ever take vacations?" she asked.

"Don't need one." Brett, the gruffer of the two, grunted. "What's that thing people say? When you work a job you love, you'll never work a day in your life?"

"Choose a job you love, and you'll never have to work a day in your life," Thatcher, the more well-read brother, corrected.

Thatcher's intelligence made him seem like he was the intellectual one, but Brett was actually the more contemplative and serious sibling. Thatcher was the goofier, sarcastic one.

Esme popped another piece of the oversized cookie into her mouth. *Pure bliss.* "You might not know this, but I do a lot of charity work, and that means event organization. I've put together a luxury vacation cruise, and I have an extra room to give away. I thought one of you might want to go. Take a well-deserved holiday."

Thatcher instantly perked up. "A cruise? Sign me up!"

Esme pressed her lips together and raised her eyebrow. "Actually, I was thinking the other brother might be interested."

"No." Brett shook his head and waved her away. "I'm not any sort of cruise guy. Don't like the idea of being locked up in a floating tin can with a bunch of strangers."

"Mostly, he doesn't like the idea of fun," Thatcher added.

"Which is why it might be good for him to go." Esme exchanged a conspiratory smile with Thatcher.

He caught on. His disappointment melted away, and he jumped on board Esme's scheming train. "You know what, she's right. You should go."

Brett, attempting to ignore them, shook his head and returned behind the counter where a label machine was printing off new orders. Thatcher followed him, and the two brothers debated in hushed tones. Esme ate her cookies, enjoying the view of the cute little town from the window.

Esme could offer this cruise to plenty of people, but she liked when things fell perfectly into place. The first piece of this particular puzzle was already set up, and she needed this one for her plan to work.

She recently started organizing cruises. It was a stroke of genius if she did say so herself. It was a great way to bring together many people from her long matchmaking list. It was especially convenient for those who lived far away from each other and were unlikely to cross paths without her intervention.

Some of the people on her list were clients who actually signed up for her services. Shifters who were patiently—though sometimes not so patiently—waiting to meet their fated mates.

Others—like Brett—hadn't signed up. They made

it on her list because they were good people who deserved happiness in their lives. It brought Esme great joy to help fate along.

"It's settled. He's going," Thatcher announced, returning to Esme's table. "I'll stay here and run the shop."

Esme glanced over to Brett, who looked none too happy about it. "How'd you get him to agree?"

"I told him that if he didn't go on this trip, then he'd have to pick another, or else I wouldn't feel free to take time off when I wanted to." Thatcher beamed with pride.

"Brotherly guilt," Esme nodded. "Smart."

"It's for a good cause." Thatcher shrugged, revealing his impish grin. "But it means I get to start looking into vacations while he's gone."

Esme squeezed his hand. "Don't put too much effort into it."

"Why not?"

She smiled mischievously. "I have a feeling something is right around the corner for you."

TWO

"I heard from Kat and Coleman," Gia announced, entering her boss's office. "They said Jaylen is settling in nicely at the new place."

The recently orphaned bobcat boy had been formally adopted by the lynx and bear—the latter a former coworker of Gia's. She'd been along on the sidelines while Kat and Coleman had fallen in love and decided to make a go of it. They would provide a stable life for the orphan. It pleased Gia to know that everything worked out.

"Good." Oren nodded and gestured toward the brown leather armchair across from his desk. "Take a seat."

She did, albeit nervously. Though she considered the man with the stern and dangerous demeanor more of a father figure than the most feared mob boss in town, she'd never been called into his office before.

"Is there a problem?" She racked her brain for anything she might have forgotten to do or mistakes, but she couldn't think of a single thing.

Gia was one of Oren's many assistants, for lack of a better term. As the head of the Cavalli bear shifter clan, Oren spread out his workers, giving each different specific tasks to ensure none were privy to too much information around his actual business dealings.

For her part, Gia was mainly a housekeeper for Oren's vacation properties. Bear clan members could borrow the locations. Her job was keeping them cleaned and well-stocked, so the families could have enjoyable trips out of town while they went up to the mountains to recharge. The cabin where Kat, Coleman, and Jaylen had stayed was one of many in the area.

Her job aligned with her career goals mostly. She studied hospitality in college and hoped to open her own bed and breakfast one day—once she saved enough to afford it.

"No problem," Oren answered. He sat back in his chair and smiled, revealing charming dimples while rubbing his short salt-and-pepper beard. "I actually wanted to thank you for a job well done."

"Uh, okay." Gia blinked in surprise. "Thanks. But,

what job? I haven't done anything out of the ordinary."

"The whole Jaylen situation. I heard that you were on the ball. Delivering food or whatever else they needed. It really helped. That kid was in a bad way, and your services made sure that Kat and Coleman could care for him properly while they were up there."

"Oh, yeah, okay." Gia wouldn't contradict her boss, even if she didn't believe she did anything particularly spectacular to deserve special praise of any kind.

She followed her job description as a cabin care-taker. She brought up what the vacationers might have forgotten and any of their last-minute whims. The only difference from her last job was that a cabin was used as a safe house for the orphaned Jaylen.

Well, that and the attack from the man who killed the parents. It didn't make her job any more difficult. Coleman dealt with all that.

"Just take the thanks!" Oren laughed. "And I'm sending you on a cruise. All expenses paid."

"You're what?" Gia slowly processed his words. "Like, for a job? Do you need me to check it out as a potential Cavalli family trip or something?"

"No, nothing like that. A friend of mine organized a cruise. Invited Anaya and me to go, but I'm too busy. I thought I'd give you the opportunity."

"Seriously?" A free vacation? From her boss?

He slid a thick invitation across the desk. Gia

picked it up in wonderment, having never seen physical travel tickets like that before. It had a QR code printed on it that would allow her to pull up all the details on her phone. *Fancy.*

"Yes, seriously. You're officially on vacation. Have fun."

Gia had a few days before the cruise to shop for vacation outfits. Cute sundresses, breezy rompers, a few floppy hats, and a different pair of sunglasses for every day onboard.

But as she shopped, the high from swiping her card was overshadowed by nagging loneliness. This would be the first vacation she planned for herself and herself alone. She traveled with friends and family before, which meant they prepared together, sharing the anticipation and excitement.

But alone? What fun would she have traveling solo? She wasn't even the kind of person who enjoyed going to movies or restaurants by herself.

You won't be alone. The boat will be full of people, she reminded herself. *You'll just have to make friends.*

On embarkation day, Gia packed a small suitcase and oversized tote bag and flew from Denver to Miami. The shuttle bus took her from the airport to Dodge Island, where she'd be boarding the cruise ship.

As she drew closer to the terminal, it became more and more apparent how huge the ship really was. She'd never seen a cruise ship in person, and it was bigger than she could have imagined. Though she'd spent time looking over the website and had learned that the vessel contained many amenities, including three pools, four casinos, loads of shops, and plenty of nightclubs and restaurants, it was something else entirely to see it in person.

Her eyes went over the crowd, moving toward the terminal building in front of the ship. She was pleased to see that while some people seemed to be traveling in families, groups, and couples, the majority appeared to be solo travelers.

Hello, bright side! That boded well for her. She might find a group to hang out with. Hopefully, a fun bunch of single ladies ready to party.

As she continued to scan her new surroundings, Gia spotted an absolutely gorgeous specimen of a man. He wore a blue sleeveless shirt over his rippling tattooed muscles, a pair of gray shorts that appeared so crisp they must be new, and a pair of aviator sunglasses that hid his eyes and accentuated his chiseled jawline. His dark hair was slicked back, and he surveyed the others around him as if he were hesitant to move forward.

He was simply a stranger in the crowd, yet her heart skipped a beat. Not in that simple *oooh, look at that hottie* way. *That* feeling she was well accustomed to. This sensation was brand new.

Why was it so intense? Why did her feet want to walk right over to him? Why did she feel like she just *had* to meet him?

She was so focused on the *why* that she didn't notice the man disappear into the crowd.

She blinked, looking frantically through the throngs of people, trying to catch sight of him again. He was gone. Nothing but a sexy mirage.

Her heart sank like she lost something very important , and a small ball of panic began to form in her chest.

Forget it, Gia told herself. Maybe it was the excitement of the vacation and the fact that... *wow.* It had been a long time since she was with a guy. Longer than she realized.

Okay, so we're going to find some singles to party with. Maybe a handsome stranger for a night or two of extra fun. Nothing wrong with that!

"Holy hotties, amiright?" a woman next to Gia commented.

The woman had medium-length red hair, a sprinkling of freckles on her nose, and wore a pretty ruffled sundress that showed off her shoulders.

Gia picked up the shifter scent, but she couldn't for the life of her figure out what the woman's animal was.

"I see your nose wrinkling," the woman laughed. "How about you tell me yours, and I'll tell you mine."

"Brown bear." Gia smiled and shrugged helplessly.

"Ah, explains it. Even shifters with a great sense of smell have a hard time pinpointing my scent. Red panda. There aren't many of us." A sad and bitter tone cut through her words. No doubt she lamented the rarity of red panda shifters.

"I'm Gia." She offered her hand.

The woman shook it. "Ray."

"Nice to meet you, Ray. Are you traveling alone?" Gia realized how that sounded. "Uh. I'm not trying to find out personal info to swindle you or, uh, worse. It's just that I'm here by my lonesome and was hoping to find some others to hang out with, so I don't have to be vacationing in solitude the whole time." She offered an embarrassed laugh, surprised at how awkward it was trying to make friends as an adult.

"It's okay!" Ray laughed along with her. "Yeah. I'm traveling solo, and I'm totally up for grabbing a drink sometime. Hit me up if you see me around deck!"

"Will do!"

They separated while they went toward the check-in desk. When Gia finished showing her ID and ticket, Ray was nowhere to be seen, but Gia figured she'd find her again sometime during the trip. Ray would be easy to find in the crowd with that bright red hair.

Gia checked her suitcase and was soon called up to

go through security, and then stood in line for boarding. She felt a little silly posing by herself for the embarkation photo, but she tried to look at it as an *empowered woman* shot. There she was, taking a vacation all alone, not letting anything stop her from enjoying herself!

She wanted to find her cabin before exploring the rest of the ship. Others seemed to have the same idea, and she had to wait in line for the elevators.

When she finally entered her room, she took inventory of her new home for the next few days. A queen-sized bed. A couch and a small table. A desk and chair with a television next to it. A bathroom so tiny it was almost comical.

At least she had a balcony. She stepped out on it, seeing she faced the ocean, not the dock, where people were still loading. She took a deep breath... and was *not* greeted with fresh ocean air. *That* was still city air.

She went back into her cabin, closed and locked the door behind her. She went through her tote, pulling out her smaller clutch and then unloading a few toiletries that she'd carried with her. She applied sunscreen, preparing herself to go back up on deck.

She noticed an itinerary on the desk. It listed the onboard activities for the day, including the sail away party that started in about a half-hour. Scanning down, she also saw scheduled singles meet-and-greets and speed dating.

Hmmm. Is that normal? She wondered. Or had Oren sent her on a singles cruise on purpose? Was her boss trying to set her up? But why? Oren didn't concern himself with his employees' love lives.

Then Gia flipped the itinerary over and spotted a large square ad with a familiar face.

Esme Baer. Matchmaker Extraordinaire.

Oh, no. Gia hadn't seen this coming, at all. Why should she have? She had no reason to think she'd be on a *singles matchmaking cruise!*

Oren mentioned a friend of his organized the cruise. *Esme* was that friend. Gia knew of her. She also knew Esme's notorious matchmaking reputation—specializing in helping shifters find their fated mates with a purported perfect track record. Gia even met the woman during the Jaylen fiasco. Actually, Esme brought the orphaned baby bobcat to Oren.

Gia now realized that Esme must have told Oren who to send up to watch over Jaylen because Kat and Coleman turned out to be fated mates.

But why would Esme target Gia next? Would Gia's fated mate be on board?

You're being silly. Maybe Esme really did just offer Oren and Anaya the trip, and he turned it down and offered it to me.

But why Gia, now? In the years she worked for him, Oren hadn't given any other employee an all-expenses-paid vacation.

Not that she knew what Oren did for his other employees. Oren was pretty secretive, such was the nature of his business. Maybe he gave out bonuses and vacations all the time, and it was just Gia's turn.

All the overthinking was starting to give her a headache. The best thing she could do would be to leave her tiny room and find what fresh air she could. She was excited to watch the ship pull away from the dock, and she knew there were special shifter-strength cocktails available up there, too.

To her delight, the moment she stepped from the interior onto the outdoor deck, she spotted Ray, her bright red hair fluttering in the breeze. She was speaking to a waiter when she locked eyes with Gia and nodded. She held up two fingers to the waiter, and he rushed away.

"I just ordered us some cocktails!" Ray called, motioning Gia to join her at the rail.

Gia blinked at the woman. She hardly knew her, but it seemed like there was trouble in her eyes that hadn't been there when they'd met earlier. "Everything okay?"

"It's fine." Ray waved her hand as though she were brushing something away. "I'm just a little nervous about being on open water, is all. Nothing a few cocktails won't fix."

Gia had a feeling that while Ray told the truth about being nervous on the open water, there was something else going on. She was too new a friend to pry, though, so she didn't ask any follow-ups.

A different waiter appeared with drinks on a tray. Gia fumbled with her clutch to find her key card, but Ray stopped her. "They're on me."

"Oh, thanks." Gia accepted the drink. She took a sip and immediately experienced the fun sensation of the momentary tipsiness it delivered before her shifter genes metabolized it all too quickly.

"Don't mention it. I'm glad for the company. Now, tell me what you think about *that* hottie."

Ray pointed to a man down the deck, and they continued to check out the eye candy until the boat started moving.

As soon as they were far enough away from the dock, the music started playing. Ray and Gia joined the other happy travelers in the sail away dance party.

CHAPTER

THREE

I can't believe I let Thatcher talk me into this, Brett thought as he filed onto the boat.

His little brother basically blackmailed Brett into taking the trip Esme offered. Thatcher insisted that if Brett didn't go on the vacation, he would feel like he wasn't free to take time off either. Considering that they'd been working together for three years with no breaks, it seemed as good a time as ever to break that trend and finally take a trip.

A damn cruise, though? Brett grumbled to himself.

This wasn't his kind of thing.

Not anymore, at least.

There was a past part of him that would love the scantily-clad women, the shifter-strength alcoholic beverages, and all the debauchery that came when you combined the two.

But now? Not so much. He'd sworn off partying when he became sober three years ago. Back when his brother basically saved his life, telling him that if he could get his shit together, then they could make a go of a childhood dream.

Brett wasn't nervous about temptation. He'd been through the program, and he'd been in plenty of situations that had tested him already. He was fine saying no to alcohol and drugs. But it did make him wonder what in the world he could do for fun on the ship. The only thing he did found enjoyable in his life now was baking. This vacation didn't include his stand mixer or an oven.

He looked at the cruise guide sitting on his cabin's desk. At least there was a sports bar. He could go there, eat fries, and cheer for his favorite teams.

There were plenty of restaurants and good food to look forward to.

There are crowds, though. Loud people. Constant chaos and the inability to find a moment to hear the thoughts in your head unless you go back to your room which is about the size of a closet.

He could get through it, though. He could deal with four days of moderate torture if it meant his little brother would go on a vacation. The kid deserved some fun.

Kid, ha. Thatcher was five years younger than Brett, but it didn't matter that Thatcher now neared thirty. Brett would always see him as his baby brother.

And he'd always want Thatcher to have a chance at a better life than he'd had himself.

Feeling claustrophobic, he left his room and walked toward the aft, taking that elevator up to the sports bar. Since most people were still touring the ship or taking part in the sail away party, the bar was almost empty.

"Hey cutie, what can I get you?" The blond waitress winked before she set a napkin down on the table in front of him.

"Just a Coke, for now, please. And some pretzels."

The waitress nodded. Brett watched different games on the televisions. When the waitress returned, she leaned close to his ear and whispered, "We really know how to party below deck after hours, if you're interested."

He stiffened. He hadn't been on the ship for a day, and already he was being propositioned. He had a feeling that her words meant more than just drinking and screwing. Did his tattoos and demeanor work as a billboard, telling people what kind of person he was?

Used to be, he reminded himself.

"Appreciate it." He nodded, looking at the TV and not her. "I'm good, though."

"Let me know if you change your mind," she said, still talking in a low voice. Then she stood and spoke in a louder, more chipper tone, "Call if you need anything else."

He watched her walk away. She had a good body, that was for sure. But he didn't want to take a chance on any of that. He stayed far away from anyone who partied hard.

After about an hour of watching the games—as well as looking out the bar's windows while the boat sailed away from the dock—Brett was bored. Cheering for sports, especially when your favorite teams weren't playing, wasn't exactly fun to do alone. The staff working in the bar weren't even watching the games. They were more interested in chatting with each other, likely talking about that night's party plans.

He left the bar and walked around the deck. Found an empty piece of railing and took a spot to look out at the water, to see the land behind them grow smaller and smaller. He never thought he'd be a wolf on the high sea, but there he was.

The deck party raged on—at least this one seemed innocent enough. People were dancing and celebrating the start of their vacation. Still, Brett was uninterested in joining. He found his way to the bow, took one of the empty lounge chairs, and just stared off to sea.

It was mesmerizing.

But he was restless. What was he going to *do* for four days?

He must have dozed off because the next thing he

knew, the sun was setting, and his stomach was rumbling. He made his way back to his cabin, pleased to see that his suitcase had been delivered, and he changed into some jeans and a clean t-shirt for dinner.

He consulted his travel documents to identify which restaurant he was assigned to for that night, and then he headed there.

When the host showed him inside, he was surprised to see that all of the tables weren't big eight or ten people tables like he'd thought they'd be. Half of the room seemed to be for groups, but the other half consisted of small two-person tables.

What kind of ship is this? He wondered. *I don't think this is normal.* Usually, cruise ships liked to pack as many people in as possible, or so he'd thought.

He walked through the restaurant with the host, and a sneaking suspicion grew in him. The people at the two-people tables all looked to be on dates. *Wait... Is this a dating cruise?*

Crap.

Was his dinner about to be a blind date? Or would he be sitting alone while everyone else had someone else to dine with?

He didn't know which was worse.

The tables were less full nearing the back of the restaurant. To his relief, many had only one person. *At least I won't be the only person dining alone.*

Then again, maybe the host was leading him to his

dining companion. Brett's eyes darted from one woman to the next, wondering which one might be his friend for the evening.

The moment he saw *her,* he knew he'd be sitting at that table.

It had to be her.

Bronze skin. Long black hair pulled into a high ponytail. Nose buried in the one-page menu like she was trying to find something to focus on. Wore a kind of coral-colored ruffly top with some white lace on it, cut into a low V that seemed to make an arrow that pointed him right toward...

Her head popped up from the menu, and she locked eyes with him. Her dark orbs captured him and drew him ever closer.

"Here you go, sir," the host said, and Brett barely had the presence of mind to thank the man while sitting across from the most alluring woman he'd ever seen.

The words of the cheesy love song streaming through the restaurant hit his ears and narrated the emotions he experienced. *Unforgettable, in every way.*

It was. *She* was. He'd remember this moment forever.

Brett nodded along to the host's recitation of the menu options for the night, impatient for him to be gone so he could learn the woman's name.

When he finally left, Brett opened his mouth to

speak as though it wasn't even his own. As if he were outside his body, watching himself bumble like a fool. "Hello there. I'm Brett."

"I'm Gia," she replied.

He felt like cotton was stuffed in his ears. Everything around him, all the chatter of the other restaurant-goers, seemed muffled. All except the clear, sweet bell sound of *Gia's* voice.

"Nice to meet you, Gia." Brett's body finally started to collect itself, gathering his senses away from doing nothing but smiling goofily at her.

What happened? He hadn't felt that way since... ever. Was he seasick?

No dummy. It's your fated mate.

The thought walloped him.

Oh no.

Fated mate? How was that possible?

And why? Why do this to him—make him meet a woman that would make him lose his senses? He didn't need such a complication in his life. All he wanted was to keep a low profile and run the bakery with his brother. Not be in the kind of situation where he would lose his wits about him over a pretty face.

He almost stood and bolted from the restaurant at the realization that she was his mate, but he breathed, making himself stay because it would be rude to make such a fine woman eat alone.

And besides, his wolf wouldn't allow it. His wolf wanted to bask in her essence.

All his internal human warnings shouted that the smartest thing he could do would be to jump overboard and start swimming to the closest nearby island.

But Brett had years of managing his urges under his belt. If there was one thing he was confident he could do, resist temptation.

CHAPTER

FOUR

And there he was.

The man she'd spotted briefly outside the terminal.

The hottest man she'd ever seen.

Her fated mate.

Walking through the restaurant, staring at her with a gaze that couldn't be described as anything less than smoldering.

His chiseled jaw set hard, his eyes locked onto her, a moment where he slid his tongue over his bottom lip and then bit it.

It took every ounce of her ability to not squirm in her seat. Instead, she took a deep breath and willed the unexpected lust to stay within.

She smiled pleasantly when Brett sat down, though inside, she hardly knew what to do. Again she wondered why Oren had sent her on the cruise. Did she seem lonely? Or had Esme decided she needed a mate?

Maybe it wasn't about her at all. Maybe it was about the guy across from her.

Maybe Esme had mysterious ways, and some might never know her motivations.

"I'm Gia." She smiled, immediately trying to break the ice with the introduction.

"Brett." His eyes were still locked on her, and he seemed to be trying to figure something out.

Probably dealing with what it means that he's just been seated with his fated mate.

"I can't decide between the oven-roasted lobster tail or the red snapper." She pointed to the items on the menu.

"I'm sure they'll bring both," Brett offered.

"I couldn't eat both..."

"Then how about I eat what you don't?" He gave her a small half-smile, and her heart fluttered. *What a man!*

They continued to talk about the menu items until the waiter came by and took their order. Then, they talked about mundane, light topics, like what they'd done on the ship so far that day.

Once their salad course arrived, Gia finally jumped into the real stuff. "So, how do you know Esme?"

"She comes into our bakery all the time."

Gia wasn't sure she heard correctly. Bakery? This big, tattooed himbo-looking guy worked at a bakery? Did he do shipping and receiving or something? Maybe they used those big 'ol muscles to stir giant vats of batter or move stacks of trays at a time.

"That makes sense," she replied. "Esme does love baked goods. What do you do at the bakery?"

"I do everything. Well, me and my brother. We opened the place a few years ago."

Though his eyes gleamed when he said it, his face quickly fell, and he looked down at his salad.

Was he embarrassed?

Gia wondered if that had to do with her first assessment of him—the fact that he didn't look the type of a bakery guy. Did he worry that she'd make fun of him?

"It's *so cool* that you run a bakery with your brother!" She made a point to let him know that he had nothing to be ashamed about. "Tell me more about it!"

"No, no." He cleared his throat, his eyes darting from the salt shaker to the butter dish. "I don't want to get into all of that." He licked his lips before pressing them shut. The man clearly didn't like talking about himself.

She wanted to press him on it, but maybe he needed some time to acclimate to being around her— *his fated mate*—before he felt comfortable sharing much more.

It was amazing how topics like the weather and their other experience traveling could take them straight through the main course and dessert before she knew it.

And, with no more food to occupy them, just one question remained.

"So, do you like dancing?"

At Gia's question, a bit of bashful blush ran back up Brett's neck, and he rubbed at it while he made up his mind.

"We're both here, right?" She added. "Stuck on this ship, so why not? Unless"—she winced, realizing she had made an assumption that since he was at the individual table with her, he was traveling alone, like she was, when he could certainly be on the ship with others, such as his brother.—"do you have a group waiting for you?

"No, I'm traveling solo," he replied with a sigh while he looked out across the restaurant.

"Me too. So, then you'll go dancing with me? Otherwise, I'll have to go in alone." She made it sound more like a request, and the alpha reacted positively to that. She knew alphas liked to provide for others, and providing her company in one of the cruise clubs seemed a reasonable ask.

She wondered what was up with him, though. Was he nervous about being around his fated mate? Had he, like her, not signed up for this and had been shocked to meet her? How was that possible, when Brett had been invited by Esme personally?

"Hey, how well do you know Esme?" she asked as they strolled out of the restaurant together. He hadn't verbally agreed to go to the club with her, but the fact that he kept step alongside her as they walked made it certainly seem like he intended to be her date for the rest of the evening.

"I've known her since we opened the bakery. Two years ago."

"Two years, huh? That's a long time." He hadn't exactly answered her question or clarified if he knew Esme was a matchmaker. "So, you knew what you were getting into when you accepted her cruise invitation?"

"I didn't want to accept the invitation. My brother made me. Used emotional blackmail, telling me if I didn't go, then he wouldn't feel like he could take a vacation either." He shook his head and smiled. There was real affection for his brother in his explanation.

They walked past the large circular-shaped windows. The night was dark, and they could make out the ripples of the ocean with the moonlight reflecting off of them.

"Right, but I mean, you knew it wasn't just an average cruise..." she prompted.

Brett's expression stayed blank.

"That Esme organized this group to set up couples?"

"Huh?" He squinted, and his head tilted in confusion.

"That Esme Baer is an intergalactically-renowned shifter matchmaker, known for finding and pairing fated mates?"

She saw realization dawning on his face. They stopped before the ship's club area entry, so they could still have enough quiet to talk.

"You didn't know?" Gia asked. "You've known her for two years, and you didn't know she was a matchmaker?"

"That... huh. That really explains it," Brett said after a moment. "I just couldn't figure out what was happening"—their eyes locked, the heat rising between them as they both silently acknowledged the attraction between them—"when I saw you."

"The fated mates thing," Gia confirmed. "Yeah, I hadn't known this was a Esme cruise until I found her name on the itinerary. My boss gave me the tickets. I thought it was just a nice little job perk or something."

"So, I mean"—he licked his lips, his eyes glued to her lips, and he took a step closer to her—"What do we do about it?"

A loud group of laughing ladies walked by them into the club area. The sound of the thrumming music made Gia's hips bounce a little. She wanted to dance. Needed a little time to get out of her head.

Had to have some time not to think about the answer to his question.

She turned back to Brett. "Would you be willing to head in and just dance for a while?"

He nodded, seeming to understand the need to let loose and not focus on the seriousness of their situation. He offered his hand, and Gia took it. He led her through the archway to the club section, a smile on his face that convinced her she was about to have a great time.

They started in the modern club, which thumped with techno mixes of current top hit songs. Gia quickly learned an important fact about her fated mate: Brett could *dance.* Though she took a few of the shifter-strength drinks before she started to feel comfortable, he didn't need any to get out onto the dance floor and show her what he was working with.

They moved on next to the nineties music club, dancing to songs they recognized from their childhoods. When they were finally sweaty and out of breath, they left and found their way to what they thought was a karaoke club, but it turned out to be a musical sing-along room.

And Gia was shocked when Brett sang along to every last word.

When they finally wanted to escape the clubs for

some fresh air, they found plenty of empty lounge chairs on the open deck. Any awkwardness between them had vanished. Gia no longer felt like her fated mate was a stranger. He felt more like a friend, someone she'd had some fun with. Someone she'd like to keep getting to know more and more with each passing minute.

They settled into the lounge chairs, their hands still interlocked, and the view of the dark sea that went on forever captured their attention. Though other couples dotted around, everyone spoke quietly, so it felt like they were alone.

For a moment, sitting there with Brett, everything seemed perfect.

"I never thought about tracking down my fated mate, you know?" Gia sighed, breaking her stare at the ocean to look instead at Brett, who was equally, if not more stunning.

Brett only grunted in reply and shrugged his shoulder slightly.

He wasn't a man of many words, but that was okay by Gia. She was known to be chatty, and Brett seemed to be a good listener. At least, he acted like he enjoyed listening to her so far.

"It's definitely something I've heard of happening," Gia continued. "I know my boss and his wife are fated mates, but it was just never something that I considered attainable for average folks. For me."

"Yeah." Brett seemed thoughtful, and Gia yearned to know what he was thinking.

But she still didn't want to pry. If he wasn't comfortable opening up to her yet, then she refused to scare him away by pushing too hard. Maybe he was still forming his thoughts on the matter like she was, and he didn't want to discuss it till he had more time to think about it.

"So, the bakery you have with your brother. What's the name of it?"

The last time she asked about the bakery, he changed the subject, so she knew it was possible he would again. This time, he surprised her by answering.

"Pastry Pack." Brett smiled widely, and Gia was relieved they could talk about him.

"Perfect name of a place run by wolf brothers." The mention of his animal was a subtle way of letting Brett know that she knew what kind of shifter he was. Though she didn't have as great a sense of smell as the canines, she was still pretty good about figuring out things like animal types—at least, on the common ones. Red panda, that was a different situation entirely.

"You should come by when we have our honey cookies. Bears like honey, right?" He raised an eyebrow, letting her know in return that he'd identi-fied her animal.

"I've never met one who didn't." Gia laughed,

pulling her legs up on the chair to curl up a little in a comfortable position, facing Brett. "What do you mean *when* you have them? Your menu changes?"

"Yeah, it's kind of our gimmick. We have some treats that are always on the menu. But we have different ones every week, so people will want to drop by and check out what's new."

"Sounds fun!"

He continued to chatter on about the bakery, and Gia basked in his enthusiasm. His deep voice was so soothing, and though it had taken some effort to encourage the man to talk, it was worth it. She could listen to him talk for hours.

When he mentioned it had only been opened for two years, she interrupted him to ask, "What did you do before opening the bakery?"

Brett's face darkened at the question, and he stared at her pensively.

Crap. She should have let him keep talking about cookie recipes. "What is it?"

Brett sighed. "This is all so new, but I guess you need to know the truth at some point if what's between us is to go anywhere."

"What truth?"

Without another word, he pulled off his polo shirt. Gia's eyes widened in appreciation at the rippling pecs and abs that proved the man had another hobby outside of the bakery—lifting weights, for sure.

However, the mood died when he turned to the side and pointed to a symbol on his upper arm. "See this?"

Gia recoiled in horror. "That's the Santibanez pack emblem."

"You know of them?"

"I do," she said gravely as she tried to catch her breath from the realization that was swirling around in her head. *This is* so *bad.* "I... I work for Oren Cavalli."

Brett had wanted the tattoo on his arm to shock her, but at the mention of Oren's name, *he* was as shocked as Gia.

He knew the same thing she did: the Santibanez wolves and the Cavalli bears were sworn enemies.

Gia knew that the Cavallis were considered the *good guys.* The Santibanez wolves were known thugs who were only out for themselves. They didn't care who they hurt on their way to more power and money. They dealt in drugs and arms, and God knows who else.

All the terrible things that Oren worked to keep *out* of their town of Idlewyld.

Gia worked for Oren, a mob boss. But *he* was on the right side of justice.

Though she knew the Santibanez wolves through reputation, she'd never met one before. And now, not only had she met one, but he was her fated mate.

"I..." Gia stood, looking around frantically, though

she didn't know what for. There were no other Santibanez wolves ready to jump out at her. No Cavalli bears ready to reprimand her for having spent time with Brett. Still, she felt everything was *wrong* in the worst ways. She'd fraternized with the enemy! "Goodnight."

She didn't shout, *and I can never see you again,* but Brett would have to understand that it was exactly what she meant.

CHAPTER

FIVE

Brett watched Gia run off, knowing it was for the best.

She didn't know that his ties with the Santibanez pack had been dissolved—everything but the tattoos he hadn't gotten removed. He refused to, clinging instead to the symbols of a past he *didn't* want to repeat.

A reminder of what his life could turn into if he didn't keep his head about him.

A part of him seized up while watching Gia's form become smaller the further away she walked from him. *She's the one. She's our mate. We can't lose her.*

No. He needed to stay away from the kind of compilations that came in packages like Gia. All he wanted was to live a quiet life, run his bakery with his brother, and never venture back to the kind of life that Gia was a part of.

She was exactly the kind of situation he needed to avoid. If she hadn't run off, would he have been able to resist the temptation? And if he didn't? If he let himself indulge in Gia, then what?

Thank goodness he'd learned about her ties to Oren Cavalli now. The idea of walking back into that life for a woman?

No.

Been there, done that.

He'd never been a smart man when it came to love. In the past, his kryptonite had been a pretty smile and the idea of finally *having it all*. His undoing had always been the idea of being with that perfect person, of connecting with the one you'd build a beautiful future with. Nothing else mattered if you went home to someone who accepted you and valued you. Someone you thought was your whole world.

He'd learned exactly how bad an idea that all was.

But we've never met our fated mate before, his wolf protested. He shook the idea from his head. The wolf saying that was the same one who'd been with him the last time he'd jumped headlong into a relationship, so how could he trust him? He didn't trust the wolf instinct, and he didn't trust his own intuition.

He trusted rational thinking and planning. Goal

setting and intentional actions. Not some *fated mate* idea that led him straight into another mob situation.

Nope.

He rose from the lounge chair, knowing she had enough of a lead that he wouldn't run into her on the way back to his room.

Before donning his shirt again, he looked down at the Santibanez emblem on his arm. He wouldn't be getting rid of it just to replace it with a Cavalli mark. Not that they'd ever accept him. They were bears, and he was a wolf with a background with their sworn enemies.

Shit. Why is this my life?

He replaced the shirt, and he saw *her* face in his mind.

Not Gia's.

Leilani's.

And not in the way he once did. Not in the way that made him feel like she was perfection on Earth. Not like when he'd thought he loved her with all of his heart.

Now when he saw the face of Leilani Santibanez, his ex-wife, he only saw her for the succubus she was. A demon sent to Earth with only one goal in mind: to find a man and use him up, then move on to the next one.

Yes, he'd fallen for the daughter of the Santibanez

mob boss, and now, he'd almost fallen for another woman involved in that world.

What were the damn odds?

BRETT TOSSED and turned all night.

He couldn't get any of it out of his head.

They would anchor off the coast of Grand Cayman Island the next day. He could pack his things, jump on one of the tenders, and catch a flight back home.

Or...

Don't do it. Don't do it.

He chanted the mantra before the thoughts could bubble to the surface. Inside of him, he knew what was going on, and he refused to entertain the thoughts, though they seemed impossible to silence.

It's different this time.

There's no way to know that.

There's no way to know it's not.

He flipped over in his bed, crushing the pillow around his head and wishing he could turn off the inner dialogue.

You were young and stupid when you married Leilani. You're older, wiser now. You make better decisions. Plus, the situation is different. She's your fated mate. If you'd have accepted the fact that Leilani wasn't your fated mate, to begin with, we never would have done all we did to prove ourselves to the Santibanez pack and win her over. We would have never married her. We would have waited. For Gia.

Back then, Brett had never thought he'd be the one lucky enough to find his fated mate. So when he'd fallen head over heels for a woman who wasn't his mate, but who was beautiful, well-connected, and made him feel like a god—just from her deeming him worthy enough to be with her—he'd jumped all-in.

He'd done anything and everything that Leilani and her father asked for. He was a good soldier and a great husband, and the deeper he went into the family, the worse he'd felt about himself. But he couldn't leave because he loved his wife.

You can't do this. You can't let what happened with Leilani stop you from making sure Gia knows the whole story. That you're not involved in the Santibanez pack anymore.

What was the point?

The point is, we're older and wiser, and she's our fated mate, and this could actually be what we're supposed to have in our lives. Besides, working for Oren isn't the same as being family—like Leilani was. You don't know. Maybe Gia is willing to walk away. Maybe Oren doesn't pretend ownership of his people like Master Santibanez does.

He stilled at that. He'd practiced telling his natural instincts to fuck off for over three years now—ever since his divorce. He focused on the bakery and stayed as honest and respectable as his brother. He wasn't used to listening to his own inclinations anymore, to giving them a chance to be correct.

The inner debate waged on all night. When he finally woke after getting a few winks of sleep, he'd made up his mind.

He wouldn't be able to go on like everything was normal if he left without coming completely clean with Gia.

He had to. It would eat away at him and give his sobriety an additional and unnecessary challenge if he didn't. He'd committed to living a life that included open communication and working on relationships. Running from a fated mate and trying to push down his feelings wasn't in line with that. No matter how petrifying it might be.

Decision made, he set out to look for Gia.

The night before, she'd told him how she'd been looking forward to visiting Sting Ray City. He hoped she hadn't changed her mind just because of his revelation.

He hurried, showering quickly, dressing, then grabbing some breakfast before loading on a tender and landing on the island.

Fortunately, he was still in time to sign up for the excursion.

The sight of her filled him with relief. She stood in a powder-blue lacy swimsuit coverup over jean shorts with a big floppy hat and oversized sunglasses. Her tan skin glistened in the sun, and her scent mixed with suntan lotion. He hadn't lost his chance to make things right with her.

He hadn't missed his chance to clear things up.

On the other hand, Gia was clearly not pleased to see him. Her eyebrows pulled together while he walked toward her, and she asked, "What are you doing here?"

"You made the stingrays sound so great last night." He tried giving her a charming smile, but it felt much too fake. He stepped closer and lowered his voice. "I needed to explain myself."

"I'm not interested," she hissed back.

"Oh, okay. So you're able to walk away from a *fated mates* situation with no lingering questions?" He threw his hands up in surrender and backed up a few steps. "Because I wanted to. I really did. But in the end, I knew it would haunt me if I just let you go."

Gia glanced around nervously at the other guests waiting for their transport to the stingrays. She stepped toward him, closing the gap so they could speak softly again. "Look, I did think about it a lot last night. You said you're a baker now, so I'm guessing you have some story about how that tattoo is old, it's in your past or something like that, but I know better. They don't let you out so easily."

"No, they don't," Brett affirmed, turning his head

off to the side while he tried to work out the best way to say it. "But if the boss' daughter tells her father that she wants a divorce and she wants her ex to be released, so she doesn't have to run into him, then they sometimes make an exception."

Gia gasped, but they had no time to continue the conversation. The small chartered bus pulled up, and passengers began to load on.

Brett gestured for Gia to board before him, and when she sat, she indicated the seat next to her as an invitation for him. They didn't continue their conversation while riding since they were surrounded by other guests and the tour guide was describing points of interest.

They couldn't talk much when they made it to the stingrays either. Brett hadn't worn his swimsuit and didn't want to rent a wetsuit, so he happily sat by the side and watched the others go into the beautiful blue water.

Though his eyes were locked onto Gia.

Wolves weren't much for water, but Gia, the woman with a bear inside, took to it happily.

Afterward, their excursion group went to a restaurant for lunch. Finally, they could restart their conversation.

"So, you were married?" Gia asked once they'd ordered.

"I was. It was a nightmare. So much so that I

thought I'd be able to watch you walk away knowing I dodged a bullet. I'd sworn off love, women, all that stuff because it had only led me to disaster."

"I see." She rested her chin on her hand and eyed him, though her face looked quizzical. The coldness from that morning had thawed a bit. "What was her name?"

"Leilani. Santibanez."

"Pretty?"

"What?" It took Brett a moment to realize that Gia's interest in his ex might be something like jealousy. He considered how he'd feel if the situation were switched, and yeah. He'd be pretty curious—*and jealous*—about any man Gia might have been married to, so he offered the information. "Yeah, I'm not going to lie. She's got the princess looks and attitude too. Used to getting everything she wanted from her father."

"What went wrong between you two? Why aren't you with her anymore?" Their waiter brought their drinks, giving them something to focus on while discussing Brett's failed marriage.

"I grew up a bit. I started to say *no* to her demands, to think that maybe a wife who supposedly loved me would support me when I refused to do things that didn't sit right with me. Turns out, she just wanted someone she could boss around."

"Oh." Something akin to sympathy passed across

Gia's face, and Brett's body suddenly sagged in a release of tension.

"So that's why I have to tell you this too. I'm not in that life anymore. Which means, even if Oren was willing to take me in, I wouldn't go back to that lifestyle. You noticed last night I wasn't drinking alcohol. It's because I'm sober. I got into some bad shit with that pack, and I want to stay away from that. It's so risky for me to be around someone who is in that lifestyle. *You're* a risk, Gia."

"I'm not in *that lifestyle*," Gia balked. "I'm a property caretaker and host, but I don't know anything that makes me *in* a lifestyle. In fact, the position I'm in has a lot of turnover. People get hired and then leave when they find something better. I work for Oren, I get a good reference, I move on to something else someday."

"Really?" Brett felt hope sprouting throughout him. "That's been your plan all along? You're not just saying that for me?"

"Why would I say that for you?" The way her tone bit let him know the question annoyed her. Likely, the whole situation did.

"Because I just said I couldn't be in that lifestyle, which means if I were to be with you, you couldn't be in that organization."

"I'm not going to hear about what I can or can't do when I don't even know what I want to do about you"

—she pointed an angry finger at him—"and me"—and then she tossed her hands up, gesturing skyward while she rolled her eyes and shook her head—"About this stupid fated mate bullshit."

Yep. She was definitely annoyed now.

Crap. So he'd cleared things up, but now he'd shoved his foot in his mouth. He came off as some kind of misogynistic brute.

How do I get myself out of this one?

CHAPTER

SIX

GIA DIDN'T KNOW WHAT SHE WAS GOING TO DO WITH this guy.

She wished she had someone to talk to. To tell her what was wise.

She didn't think he'd told her any lies. She believed that he was over his ex, but she still didn't like the idea of hooking up with Leilani Santibanez's ex-husband. Divorce or no divorce, shifters felt possessive about what was once theirs.

But he never should have been hers. He is ours, her bear growled inside her.

She had to calm down. She was snapping at Brett about her job stuff when really, she was over-the-top jealous about some woman she'd never met.

No, it wasn't the jealousy. Sure, that was there, but what she was actually pissed about was the hurt in

Brett's eyes when he revealed that Leilani had only wanted him when he obeyed her commands.

That bitch.

She tried to focus on the fact that Brett had been young and made mistakes, and he'd made something better of his life.

But she couldn't shake the anger she had toward his ex. *How dare she use him like that?*

Well, he'd already survived one unhinged woman, so Gia had to get herself in control. She excused herself from the table, went to the washroom to relieve herself then splashed cold water on her face.

As she was drying off, a familiar face walked in.

"Whoa, Ray! Small world!" Gia joked. They were all on the same cruise ship with nearly a thousand people on board, and other cruise ships had also let off thousands of people, but she couldn't have felt more relieved to meet up with the closest thing she had to a friend on her vacation.

"How's everything going? Ray asked. "Did I see you chatting with a real hunk out there?"

"Fated mate, can you believe that?" Gia muttered. "Too bad he comes with a load of baggage that I'm not sure if I can deal with."

Ray's eyebrows flew up and her mouth rounded. "That *suuuucks...*"

"Would you date a criminal?" Gia blurted out.

"Not if he were a *current* criminal," Ray replied.

"Wait. Robin Hood was a criminal, right? I'd date him. So if it were for the right reasons, I guess my answer is, yeah."

"Not a current criminal. Just, well, a crappy past."

"Oh, in that case, I definitely wouldn't write someone off for that. We all do shit in our past, but that's why we shouldn't let it define us."

Gia nodded, hearing the rightness in Ray's words. "And if he had an ex that treated him like shit, and you're pretty sure you'd beat her ass if you saw her?"

"Then call me for backup if you need it." Ray laughed. "Seriously though, I'm guessing this ex isn't his fated mate? Unless it's supposed to be a trio thing." Ray shrugged.

Nothing wrong with triads, but the idea of a triad with *Leilani*? Gia shuddered. "No! God, no. It's not a triad. She's an ex. A non-fated mate ex who he doesn't want anything to do with."

"Then I don't see any problem. Sounds like you can move forward with the person he is now, knowing he gained knowledge and experience from his past mistakes."

"You're kind of wise, red panda lady. Thank you."

"Ha! Well, if you want real wisdom, then I'll tell you that you better not let any of this drama stuff stand in your way of having a good roll in the hay with this guy. Sex with fated mates is better than anything, and you're on vacation to have a good time, right?"

They spoke for just a bit longer before Gia excused herself, not wanting anyone to come searching for her or think she bailed.

Forget about Leilani. Let's focus on Brett.

When Gia returned to the table, she managed a fresh smile. "Alright. That was a lot to take in, but I'm good now."

He gave her a relieved half-grin. "So, are there any skeletons in your past you want to share? To even the playing field, so to speak?"

She laughed. "Nope, sorry! I had a pretty normal childhood, went to college for hospitality, and was referred to the job with Oren by a family friend. I have spent my time saving up my money to open a bed and breakfast someday."

He perked up at that. "A bed and breakfast? That's interesting."

"I think so!" she agreed. "I like the idea of a cozy little place people can sneak off to."

They made it through lunch and afterward went with the tour group down to the shopping district. Brett stayed by her side the whole time, not complaining about shopping and even finding some things for himself.

All in all, it was a perfect afternoon.

When they tendered back to the boat, they agreed they'd see each other for dinner. Gia still had no idea how her boss would react to her being fated mates with a former Santibanez wolf, but she had days until she had to worry about that.

She showered and changed into a flowy boho below-the-knees beach dress in a sunset ombre and nude strappy sandals. She added long teardrop earrings and let her long dark hair down for the evening, though she usually wore it pulled up in a ponytail.

Yeah, she may have thought *I'm getting lucky tonight,* on her way out the door, but Ray was right. She was on a cruise to have fun, after all. She might not know what would happen when they left the ship, but she did know that she wouldn't want to miss out on having sex with her fated mate. Ray had said it, and she'd heard it from others before, too: sex with fated mates was better than any other sex. Why let the chance pass her by when it's right there?

In such a muscular, drool-worthy package.

They were assigned to a different restaurant that night, and now that they'd come to know each other a bit more, things were a little less awkward than dinner had been the previous night. At least Brett was more open and chatty. They discussed the food options, and he got on a roll, talking about food and cooking and baking.

After dinner, they opted to go to one of the shows in the theater instead of dancing again. Gia figured it would be best because she was pretty sure that grinding on the dance floor would just lead to them ending the night early—in one or the other's bed.

She hadn't expected the Broadway-style show to set the stage for a tantalizing two hours in the dark with Brett. What started as innocent hand-holding moved to hands rubbing on thighs, fingers tickling the back of the neck, whispers that sent tingles through her whole body, and more. Waiting through the entire show filled her with anticipation while her desire for Brett grew and grew. She wanted him... and *now*.

The torturous minutes ticked on until the show ended, the floor lights turned on, and the audience began to slowly file out of the theater. Row after row of people ahead of them moved. All Gia could think was that it would be faster to wait for everyone to leave and just jump Brett right there.

Of course, she didn't do that. But when Brett used the crowded aisle to press in close to her, rubbing her ass while pressing his hard cock against her, she had to bite her lip to stay focused.

They exchanged knowing looks and headed to the elevator. The time for small discreet touching was over. They each had the same goal in mind now.

There were too many people in the elevator for them to fool around, and she ended up giggling like a schoolgirl when she snuck a glance and caught the way he stared at her. Had she ever been so giddy for sex before? She didn't think so.

Being with him really was better than anything she'd felt in the past. Her entire body seemed to light up with his touch, and she couldn't wait to see what it was like to go all the way.

She led him off the elevator and back to her room, acting casually, which felt like it was just part of the game of tension they were playing. Brett leaned against the wall while Gia used her keycard to open the door, and then he followed her into the room, shutting the door behind them.

Alone at last, they silently stared at each other. Though she'd become used to the gentle rocking of the boat, it swayed her tonight. Perhaps it was her passion for Brett that made her head spin, shaking up her unsteady legs. She stumbled a little when she took a step toward him.

He reached out to steady her.

"Want to go to the balcony for some fresh air?" Gia suggested.

"Sure."

She opened the balcony door and stepped outside, leaning against the rail to peer out at the water.

Brett stepped behind her, wrapping his arms around her waist and resting his chin on her shoulder. They breathed in the salty air and admired the waves, both sensing the change in their embrace. He gently brushed her hair back and kissed her neck. He followed a tantalizing line to the strap of her dress.

With a moan, she leaned back into him, letting his lips work around her collarbone, and his hands explore her waist, her stomach, her breasts.

She gasped in pleasure when his fingers grazed over her nipples.

That was enough. She couldn't take it anymore. She tugged him back into the room, closing and locking the balcony door and pulling the curtains closed, though no one could possibly see them inside. There was nothing but ocean as far as you could see.

She dropped her dress, stepping out of it toward him, wearing only her sandals, underwear, bra, and earrings.

He sucked in a breath. "You're absolutely amazing."

"I'd like to return the compliment," she teased. "But you have me at a disadvantage."

It was all she needed to say for him to remove his polo shirt and drop his dark-wash jeans to the ground. "Better?"

She bit her lip and walked forward, rubbing her hand down his many rows of abs. "Much."

And then they were in each other's arms, kissing and discarding their remaining clothes and shoes that stood between them and glorious nakedness.

Their bodies pressed together hotly, grinding desperately until they found the bed. There was no extra buildup, no extra teasing. Waiting as long as they did had been enough foreplay.

The moment they united was everything Gia had hoped for. Pure bliss.

She was certain that if that night was the only one she could spend with her fated mate, well, it wouldn't be enough. At least it was an absolutely perfect memory that would last her a lifetime.

CHAPTER

SEVEN

Brett woke up in Gia's bed, feeling more peaceful and at home than he had in his entire life.

His arms were wrapped around her. He'd held her all night. Her warmth, her softness, her scent all gave him the certainty that he was *exactly* where he was supposed to be.

Too bad it had to end when she awoke and revealed that she had a full spa day ahead of her.

"I can cancel it if you want to—"

"Don't you dare," Brett said. "It's still your vacation. You deserve a massage and whatever pampering they'll give you."

Which meant that after breakfast, he had a whole day of not seeing his beautiful Gia until dinner.

Having not had a workout for a few days, Brett

decided to go to the onboard gym. There were several others in there, crowding the treadmills and weights.

He started with some squats and lunges and was about to move onto some arm work when a voice called out to him.

"Hey, can you give me a spot?"

Brett turned to see a man sitting on the weight bench.

"Sure thing." Brett walked over and introduced himself, shaking his new buddy's hand. He learned that the man's name was Bill.

He didn't want to stare, so he stayed focused on the barbell and weights, but he thought there was something different about Bill, that perhaps he had some... enhancements.

Was Bill a cyborg?

Brett kept the question to himself, though.

The man did a set of reps and then asked for more weight. Again. And again.

"Got a lot on your mind?" Brett asked since it seemed clear that Bill was trying to work something out.

"How can you tell?" The man asked.

"Just a general, *I'm going to punish my body,* workout rather than a nice *let's workout for fun on vacation* vibe about you."

The man grunted, replaced the barbell, and finally sat up.

"It's just"—Bill sighed and rubbed his face—"every time you think you have your shit figured out, life turns around and shows you that you don't, you know?"

Brett barked out a loud laugh. Loud enough he drew looks from the other gym-goers. He waved his hand, signaling his apologies for disturbing them, but at least he'd managed to make Bill crack a grin.

"So you know what I mean."

"Do I ever." It's how he'd felt since the moment he laid eyes on Gia and realized that the world was laughing at his plan for an excitement-free future.

They swapped places, and Bill spotted Brett. They worked out in silence, besides Brett's grunts and the sound of the bar going back in the rack. They didn't elaborate on their individual troubles but enjoyed their new friendship built on commiserating.

Bill left when Brett finished his reps, and Brett hopped on the treadmill, facing the endless ocean while running. With Bill gone, though, he had to face the thoughts he'd been avoiding.

He really, *really* liked Gia. Every moment he wasn't with her, he thought about seeing her again. And the sex?

God. Being with her was like nothing he'd ever experienced.

What's going to happen when we disembark? When

we step off the boat and head back toward our regular lives?

He forced himself to believe that he'd find a way to deal with it if Gia told him she wanted to go their separate ways. He'd think about her every day for the rest of his life, but he was strong. He'd worked on being emotionally and mentally resilient, and he'd survive it.

But maybe you don't have to. Maybe you should talk to her, tell her that you'd like to see this through.

That was too much to think about. It was much easier to believe he would have to forget her than it was to open himself up to the hope that it might actually work out.

He arrived nice and early for dinner—before the restaurant had even started seating folks. He wanted to be early, to enjoy every second he could with Gia.

He stood in line, waiting his turn to be seated, and he thought he saw someone. His ice froze in his veins. *No!* He looked again, blinking his eyes to clear them. Had he really seen what he thought he did?

No. It must have been a figment of his imagination.

He pushed that strange idea from his head. Once the host seated him, Brett looked over the meal choices for the evening, looking up every now and then to see if Gia had arrived yet.

Then that damn apparition appeared again.

Tawny skin like Gia, but shorter. Dark hair like Gia, but cut shoulder-length and curly, making it look like a circular frame around her face.

And very much unlike Gia, this phantom had a face much harsher, with a pointed chin, sharp nose, and lips pulled into a scowl.

It took him a moment to realize that it was no phantom. It was *actually* his ex-wife sauntering over him on the cruise ship, wearing a short sparkly black dress with some kind of crazy pointed sleeves that made it look like she wore shoulder armor or something.

The fuck is she doing here?

Leilani walked straight up to his table and took the seat across from him.

"Hello, husband."

"Ex-husband," Brett growled. "What the fuck are you doing here, Leilani?"

"Well, you know I keep tabs on you, sweets. And my little birdies let me know that you were going on a Esme Baer matchmaking cruise. You can imagine my surprise. You should have asked me before coming here."

"No," Brett spat out, holding his temper, though he internally fumed. How could she sit there and act like she had any say in what he could or couldn't do? "I didn't know it was a matchmaking cruise. Not that it would have made a difference in whether or not I *asked your permission.*"

"Mates are for life." She shrugged nonchalantly, glancing at the wine menu like she intended to make herself comfortable there with him.

"Not when they are annulled by the pack alpha at his daughter's request," Brett reminded her.

"The dissolution meant *I* was given certain freedoms, Bretty. It didn't mean that *you* did. I rank higher than you, in pack life and real-life—"

He winced at the nickname. It had been cute when he thought they were in love. Now it just sounded like she was calling him *Betty.*

"I don't live on pack lands. I'm not part of the pack. And my personal life is outside of Santibanez control as well. You're overreaching Leilani, and you know it. Though you might try to play alpha, you're not one. Especially not over me. Not anymore."

He was an alpha in his own right. He'd played beta to her while he was dumb enough to think he loved her, but he'd grown out of that a long time ago.

"It doesn't matter how far away you go. We'll always be connected." Leilani shrugged and then raised her hand to call over a waiter. Brett grabbed her hand and pulled it back down.

"You're not ordering anything. You're leaving." The only thing stopping him from putting her in her place was the fact that she *did* have certain protections, being the daughter of the Santibanez alpha and mob boss. If he caused a scene and embarrassed her, he'd be embarrassing Mr. S, and that could be asking for trouble.

"Not without you, I'm not."

"Why do you *care*, Leilani?" Brett finally asked. "We're divorced. A mutual decision, remember? You didn't want me anymore."

"And I don't want you now, either," she replied. "But divorce or no divorce, you're mine. My *ex,* sure, but the *mine* is still there. I keep tabs on you. So far, you haven't been dating, but I knew it would happen eventually. I figured if I approved, it would be fine."

She shrugged nonchalantly and brought a palm to her curls, scrunching them like they were more interesting than her conversation with Brett. "Imagine my surprise when I learned this woman you're trouncing around with is a Cavalli bear? *Nooooo.* That won't do. How would that look on me? A Santibanez wolf discarded for a Cavalli bear? Not okay."

A third voice popped up. "Well, you don't have a say in any of it." Brett had been so wrapped up in his fury toward Leilani that he hadn't seen Gia approach the table.

Leilani's face turned menacing, and she whipped to look toward Gia. "There are so many accidents that happen on boats and in foreign countries, you know? And I don't have to point out how I clearly have the connections to board the ship so many days into the itinerary. So, you can see, the sky's the limit when I set my mind on something."

"That's enough," Brett growled, rising and grabbing Leilani by the arm. "You won't touch her."

"I won't, as long as she's not involved in my life. And being in *your* life means being in mine."

The threat froze his heart. Getting close to Gia had placed her in Leilani's sights, and he didn't want to find out what lengths his ex would go to ensure she got what she wanted.

Seeing his face fall, Leilani crooned, "Ahh, good boy. You understand what it means. Well, tell your little plaything goodbye. And, you remember Niall, don't you? He's one of my daddy's best personal bodyguards. Just so you know, he's here with me, watching to make sure *I* don't fall into any trouble." She waved to the wall of a man in a three-piece suit standing by the doorway.

Leilani looked Gia up and down and sneered. "Nice meeting you, *Gia.*"

Brett couldn't look at Gia while he left the table, marching out of the restaurant with Leilani and her bodyguard. He had to figure out what to do about this, but the only thing he knew for sure was that he had to do whatever was necessary to protect Gia from his unhinged ex.

CHAPTER
EIGHT

Left alone at the table, Gia took a seat where Leilani Santibanez had just been and blinked in shock. She vaguely noticed the people around her looking in her direction and murmuring, but it made no difference to her.

She wondered if Brett would return, but she felt it in her soul that he wouldn't.

Leilani threatened Gia, and that was something Brett wouldn't risk.

The waiter approached the table, acting as though he hadn't seen the entire encounter. He offered to take her wine order. She told him what plate she wanted and that he could probably take away the second setting. To his credit, he acted completely pleasant and like nothing was wrong.

She stayed through the whole meal, even ordering dessert though she only ate a few bites.

As she'd suspected, Brett didn't return.

They'd been on the late dinner seating that day, so by the time she went out to the deck, it was dark and nearly empty. She found her way to the pool bar that served shifter-strength cocktails and started ordering.

She wasn't sure how many drinks she'd downed before someone sat in the lounge chair next to her.

"Hello, Gia."

"Hello, *Esme,*" Gia replied bitterly. Here was this woman, meddling in people's lives, and for what? One night of sex with a fated mate, she supposed. Maybe that's all she'd ever have, and she'd just have to be happy with that.

"What are you doing out here by yourself?" Esme asked.

"Drinking away my troubles," Gia said, making a great showing of holding up her neon-pink cocktail for Esme to see. "Awful fun to come on a shifter boat and get these strong shifter drinks."

"I mean, where is Brett?"

"With his wife," Gia answered.

"His *wife*?" Esme's voice went high, and her mouth rounded. Clearly, she was shocked to hear the news.

"You didn't know he was married?" Gia laughed. With a mutter, she added, "And here I thought Ms.

Esme Baer knew everything about everyone." Gia slurped her drink and a small hiccup escaped her.

"He's *not* married," Esme corrected, proving Gia's point about her knowing everything about everyone. "But my shock here stems from the fact that Leilani is *here*? On *this* boat?"

"Live and in the flesh. Apparently, the 'ex' part doesn't mean she's stopped stalking him. And she doesn't approve of him moving on with a Cavalli bear like me. I mean, I highly doubt she'd approve of him being with *anyone* else. Maybe a mouse. Someone who would be scared of her. Someone who would let her come in and out of his life and boss him around."

"And you wouldn't do that."

"Of course, I wouldn't. Oooh, I should have just beat her ass right there." Gia slapped her armrest for emphasis.

Esme ignored Gia's threats toward Leilani. "And what do you think Brett needs? A mouse? Or a bear?"

"Brett needs"—Gia scrunched up her face as she tried to think of the right words—"I don't know, to grow a pair and tell his wife where to shove it?"

"Ex-wife, and you don't think he would? He's an alpha. If he didn't put her in her place, then there was a reason. What was it?"

"Because *that woman* was making threats on me. You should have seen his face, Esme. Someone basically says she's going to make me disappear, and it was like *poof!* All his confidence and bravado were gone. Big guy like that, and it all goes away because of her. He ushered her right out of there."

"And what? You just sat there like a mouse? You didn't stand up and shout, *bring it?*" Esme asked.

"No," Gia replied with a bit of chagrin.

"So you both let each other down?"

"Yeah."

Esme looked at the pink concoction in Gia's cocktail glass, watching the liquid move from side to side from a combination of the boat's mooring as well as Gia's own wobbliness. Esme stood, plucking the glass from her hand. "I think you've had enough. Maybe it's time you go make things right."

"Oh no." Gia nestled onto the lounge chair, showing she was content to stay there all night if she wanted to. "I'm not going to go there and find him all making up with his ex."

"You know he's not." Esme tossed Gia's bag on her lap. "You saw how she treated him. Now imagine her treating a young, dumb, in-love version of Brett like that. Imagine what she might have been able to convince him to get into, to do. Now, he's older and wiser and can protect himself from her. You are a new situation for him, and though he can defend himself from Leilani, he doesn't know what she might do to you. So you need to show him that you're not some helpless damsel he needs to protect. You need to go to him and tell him that you can protect yourself and that neither of you have anything to fear from his ex."

Esme's words sank in, and suddenly fury rose in Gia. She stood. "Yeah! You're right! We're *fated mates*! We're *in this together!* And besides, I might not be a polar bear, but if she tosses me overboard, brown bears are almost as good at swimming!"

"That's the spirit," Esme said a little tentatively. "How are you feeling? Is this the alcohol talking? Maybe you need a min—"

"No, you know that even shifter strength alcohol hardly affects bears unless we drink it continuously. I'm good. You've helped me to see the light. Ain't no *Santibanez wolf* gonna tell me who I can and can't be with!"

Esme gave her Brett's room number and wished her luck.

The shifter alcohol continued to fade from her system while she walked to the elevator. As it took her down, the enormity of her situation set in.

He's a wolf. An ex-Santibanez wolf soldier.

He has a crazy ex stalking him, who happens to be connected to one of the most powerful crime families and an enemy of my boss.

Would Leilani stop if Gia stood up to her? No. Gia knew the type well enough to know they'd escalate. If Leilani couldn't control Gia and Brett directly, she'd come at it from another direction.

The bakery. His brother. They could be at risk. People like Leilani burned things down for fun. She knew too many stories of deranged people doing unthinkable things.

But that was just it. Leilani wasn't going to stop at Gia. Maybe this was the first time Leilani re-entered Brett's life since the divorce, but now that she knew she had some power and pull, she could do anything she wanted at any time. She was probably celebrating the fact that she now had Brett under her control again.

Gia staying away wouldn't do any favors to Brett. It would actually do worse.

Nope. She left the elevator, relieved her body metabolized the alcohol quickly. She was resolved. She would go to Brett and tell him that she wasn't going to leave him on his own.

And if Leilani was there when Gia showed up? Gia scoffed. *Good luck to her.* Because Gia might not be drunk, but she didn't need to be to kick ass.

BRETT CRINGED at the knock on his door. Sure, of course, ex-wife had found him. She *did* have the resources, after all.

The thing was, what could she want? It wasn't *him.* That much was clear.

When they were younger, she'd enjoyed the sex. She'd enjoyed having a younger man worship her, let her be in charge.

But as he'd grown and matured and moved into his more alpha personality, she'd hated it. She didn't want to be with a strong man. They were absolutely sexually incompatible by the end of their marriage.

So if the ex-wife wasn't showing up for sex, what was she showing up for? To make more threats? Why? He said he wouldn't see Gia anymore, so what else could she possibly want to discuss?

There was only one way to find out what Leilani wanted.

He rose from his bed and went to the door.

To his surprise, Gia stood on the other side.

"Is that bitch inside?"

"What? No." Brett had to leap out of the way when Gia pushed her way in, nearly shoving him into the wall in the small quarters. "What are you doing here?"

"Look, I should have told your ex what-for at dinner." Gia ignored his assurance that Leilani wasn't there, looking in the closet, bathroom, and through the room before she finally took a seat on his bed. "I was too shocked, I guess. But now that I thought about it, she can't tell us what to do."

"Have you been drinking?" he asked.

"A little, yeah, but it's fine. I have my wits about

me. It's more and more out of my system by the minute."

"Well, then hopefully, you'll come to your senses." His whole being yearned to sit next to her, to wrap his arm around her, to feel her close, but he knew what a threat Leilani posed. They couldn't challenge her. She'd hurt Gia, and he couldn't let that happen. "You shouldn't be here. We shouldn't see each other anymore. Leilani isn't someone to mess around with. She will make good on her threats."

"And what? You're just going to live life like that? Letting her pop in and demand this or that, knowing she can hurt you or people you care about? You'll kowtow to her demands, you'll never get close to anyone because she gets to boss you around? She knows she can, after tonight. Boss you around, that is."

He hadn't considered that. He'd only thought that Gia was a once-in-a-lifetime event. A fated mate. Everyone only gets one—unless they're meant to be in a triad or quad or more. He figured that when he turned his back on Gia, Leilani would have what she wanted, and that would be it.

But what Gia said made sense. Leilani had a taste now of controlling him again, and it wouldn't be long till she was back, telling him to do something else.

He'd stepped onto a slippery slope leading straight back toward the Santibanez pack.

Right where Brett didn't want to be.

"So, then what do you suggest?" he sighed and rubbed his forehead. He was tired of thinking, tired of trying to figure out what to do about a woman he thought he'd been free of.

Gia patted the bed next to her, and he sat. She snaked her arms around his neck and pressed her forehead to his. "I know you spent years being chewed up by this woman, and you've had a few years to breathe, and seeing her tonight would have been miserable. But you're not who you were when you first met Leilani. And Leilani"—Gia ran her fingers through his hair and breathed in deeply—"she's full of hot air, whether she knows it or not."

Brett touched Gia's face, feeling relief at her mere presence. He kissed her, feeling his resolve improving.

"I was young. I wanted love. I thought I'd made it when a girl like her, the alpha's daughter, the boss' daughter, wanted me. But it was all bad." Brett pulled away, looking off to the side of the room, the shame of his past decisions haunting him once again.

"Sometimes we go through bad things while we're trying to find the good." Gia kissed his jaw while she spoke. "But her re-appearing doesn't mean you're back there. You're in a better place now. And you have someone at your side who sees you for *you*. Who wants you to have the life of your dreams. Not someone who only sees you for what you can do for them."

Her words gave him hope.

Making love to her that night gave him the certainty that he could never turn his back on his fated mate.

He would fight for her.

No matter how choppy the sea.

CHAPTER
NINE

Gia and Brett pushed Leilani out of their minds and focused on enjoying their last day of vacation.

This was a particularly special day since the boat was docking at a pair of privately-owned islands. Shifter onboard had a special invite to go to a secret island, where they could spend the day in their animal form. They could bring their non-shifter mates or traveling buddies—as long as they were aware of the existence of shifters. Human cruise goers would go to the other island and would have no idea that the second one was even an option.

"It says most of the inside island is covered in a canopy of trees, and there are formations around the island that prohibit strange boats from coming too near. There's also tech set up to block drones and cell signals and the like." Gia commented.

"There would have to be," Brett reasoned. "I'm sure they're very careful. A secret shifter island is a great boon for them, and if it were ever compromised, they'd lose a big swath of their shifter vacationers."

They arrived on the island, checking their clothing into lockers and then shifting and running free. All around her, Gia spotted different animals. Mostly the big common ones—wolves, bears, lions, and tigers—but the smaller ones were there, too. She watched a raccoon, a fox, and even a black cat scurry by.

In the distance, she could see an area where folks in human form mingled.

As she ran along, investigating the woods, she acknowledged every other bear she passed. It was strange. She'd grown up in the Cavalli lands and hadn't known many other bears outside of them, so it was fun to see stranger bears and connect with them so far from home.

After the initial elation of running in her animal form, she finally stopped, turned, and took a good look at Brett in his wolf form.

He was a large gray wolf. Enormously so. As big, if not bigger, than her bear form, although he wasn't quite as large as the largest bear she knew, his size was still impressive. She wouldn't want to fight him, that was for sure.

His underside was almost white, and his back coat was a dark pepper gray, spreading down his face like a mask that went over his nose but left his cheeks and bottom jaw white.

His eyes, though. Amber-colored now, instead of his normal sienna, they looked at her with the softness of someone who truly cared.

A few things occurred to Gia then. One, Brett probably had never run with a bear before—she'd certainly never run with a wolf before. A lynx, yes, now that Nila was mated to Pryce, but never a canine.

Two, it had probably been a long time since Brett had shifted with *anyone* outside of his brother.

To break the awkwardness of the moment, seeing how Brett seemed to have no idea what to do, Gia chuffed at him and lumbered forward, gently head-butting him. He stumbled a little, looking shocked, and she circled him, making a little growl to encourage him.

He huffed in acknowledgment and trotted forward, then looked back as though unbelieving that she was really going to follow him.

But she did.

They ran through the center of the island, the wooded part, and when they were finally exhausted, they found the beach, where many other animals had found their way. As the line of trees thinned, the ground turned to soft sand. Brett's wolf halted before his feet touched the water, but Gia barreled forward, enjoying the strange sensation of saltwater soaking her bear fur.

He watched her from the shore until she was completely soaked, refreshed, cooled off, and then she made her way back to him, nuzzling against him—and amusing herself by making his coat wet. Then they laid together on the sand, on the paradise-like beach full of other shifters in their animal forms—and some with their mates in human forms—watching the ocean roll in.

Gia's fur was finally dry when it was time for lunch. There were two options. Shift into human form and partake in the buffet, or stay in your animal form and eat the raw food options.

Though she loved fresh fish, she wanted a chance to chat with Brett. The morning had been quiet. She wondered if after they had properly mated —*if* they did—if they'd be able to talk through the telepathic link. She wasn't sure. Some could only do that through a pack link, and if she left the Cavallis, would she lose her link with them and make a new one with her mate?

Either way, they went back to the area with their lockers, shifted and changed into clothes. As they stood in line at the buffet, his hands never strayed too far from her. They loaded their plates and ate together while chatting about the perfect island afternoon.

They both agreed they'd take another cruise here in a heartbeat.

After lunch, they walked for a bit on the human path, holding hands. But Gia didn't want to waste the opportunity.

"What do you say, another shift and run before we're back on the boat?"

Brett agreed, and they once again placed their clothes in the lockers, shifted, and ran.

There were fewer animals now, as people were eating, lounging on the beach, or headed back to the boat.

Gia and Brett began to race. The wolf would definitely beat her, so she made it her mission to take the lead. When she finally did, she made the most of it, barreling forward with a celebratory roar.

She'd expected him to quickly catch up and pass her, and when he didn't, she looked behind her.

Brett wasn't there.

She halted, looking in all directions. *Where is he?*

She turned around, about to head back to look for him, when a different gray wolf stepped out in front of her.

This one was still large but smaller than Brett and much smaller than Gia. Her fur was white underneath, but the top gray was light, almost silver. She'd be quite beautiful if her lips weren't pulled back into a snarl.

Leilani.

There was no time to try to reason with her. The wolf instantly attacked. Gia would have been caught off-guard if her bear instincts hadn't been ready for it. It had felt the danger, recognized the wolf, and braced for the impact all before Gia's human mind could be prepared for it.

Wolf and bear fought, snapping and striking, their growls, yips, and roars drawing attention. The wolf was vicious and faster than the bear. Leilani had the motivation and drive to take the bear down, but Gia didn't have the same desire to cause harm. She only wanted to thwart the wolf's efforts.

Which Gia mostly did, using her strength and size advantage to swat the bear and headbutt her away. She thought she was doing fairly well until she saw the red blood on the wolf's fur.

And it wasn't because Gia had drawn the blood.

Gia didn't have time to look herself over and see where Leilani had injured her. She had to rely on her shifter healing ability to patch herself up quickly. Now it was clear that her simple defensive moves weren't going to do anything to stop the wolf. The only way Leilani would stop advancing was if Gia took the wolf down.

Ugh.

Gia hadn't been in a fight for her life like this. But it was clear that's what Leilani wanted. Luckily, Gia had been raised in a bear clan that often practiced fighting, in case this day ever came.

And the moment Gia went on the offensive, it was clear that Leilani, the pack princess, hadn't had the same upbringing.

Leilani didn't know how to dodge blows. She wasn't expecting Gia's speed, which was slow compared to wolves, and should have been something Leilani easily outmaneuvered.

Gia realized that if Leilani had any training at all, her sparring partners must have pulled punches. Had the wolf's alpha daddy told everyone to go easy on her? Or was it just that she had no training at all?

Gia hated the sounds the wolf made as she was pummeled, but every time Gia stepped back to allow the wolf to run away, the wolf refused to quit.

Stupid girl.

"Step back, or we'll shoot!" The shouted words barely go through to Gia, and she glanced up to see a security team surrounding them, guns pointed.

Though she knew she was leaving herself open to Leilani, she had to do the right thing. Gia instantly sat up, raising her front two bear paws in the air to surrender.

The wolf wasn't as wise. She took the moment of Gia's stillness to lunge.

And a tranquilizer dart caught her in midair.

"Ma'am, you've broken the rules of the island by

engaging in combat. Please shift in to your human form, or we'll be forced to incapacitate you."

Gia didn't need any more prompting. She shifted and accepted the bathrobe they offered. Two security guards escorted her back to the main building with her, taking her statement as they walked.

"It wasn't my idea. I was just defending myself," Gia explained, scanning the area for Brett. *Where is he?*

"Our job isn't to determine who is at fault. It's just to break up conflicts and remove those involved," the first guard informed her.

"They'll review the footage, and if your story checks out, they'll let you go with no problem," the other guard added.

"Footage?" Gia asked.

"Oh yeah, we have security cameras all over the place. The footage doesn't leave the island, but we need some way to keep tabs on our guests for situations just like this."

"What happens to the aggressor?"

"She'll be shipped home immediately and banned from future cruises."

Gia figured that sounded like a fair punishment. Though she needed to look herself over closely, it seemed like all she had was a few scratches that were already healing.

"Gia!" Brett, in his human form, ran toward her from the main building.

"Where were you?" Gia called back. "What happened to you?" Not like she'd needed his backup, but she just wondered how they'd been separated and why he never showed back up.

"Someone put in a false report. Security stopped me and made me come back for questioning and to inspect my locker for contraband. I'm cleared, of course, but"—he paused, concern growing on his face as he finally noticed the security guards on either side of her.—"what happened to you?"

"Ah, that Leilani." Gia shook her head. "She thought of it all. She took you out of the picture and attacked me in the woods. I'm being removed for fighting."

"What?"

"Sir, you're going to have to move aside," the first security guard interrupted.

"But, we're together, can't I go—"

"No, you'll have to return to the boat with the rest of the passengers and claim your travel buddy from the brig once you're on board."

"It's okay, I'm fine," Gia assured him. "Boat jail isn't real jail, and they have cameras in the woods. They'll review it and see that *she* was the aggressor and I was just defending myself."

Brett looked aghast at letting her walk away, but there was nothing either could do about it.

CHAPTER

TEN

SECURITY ALLOWED GIA TO COLLECT HER THINGS AND change into her clothes before they loaded her onto the security tender, which took them through a special entrance to the cruise ship.

Leilani was still unconscious from the tranq, but she'd turned back into her human form, and someone had thrown a bathrobe on her.

Security kept the two women separated on the tender, even though Leilani didn't wake up the whole ride. She didn't wake up once they were in the brig either. They had to place her on a stretcher and carry her inside.

The small brig, the cruise boat's jail cell, didn't have iron bars like Gia assumed jails had. Instead, it was a small padded room with a bed and a door to a tiny bathroom with a toilet, sink, and shower.

She heard Leilani the second the other woman woke up. She shouted through the walls, making all kinds of threats.

"I told him to stay away from you! I told him he'd regret it."

Gia rolled her eyes. She was sitting on the bed, her legs pulled up. She shook her head and rested her forehead on her knees. *I'm already so sick of this woman.*

"I know you can hear me, bitch."

"Leilani, chill," Gia finally shouted back. "Did you really not learn your lesson? Had security not intervened, I would have torn you up. You really want to try me again?"

Wrong thing to say. Leilani went on a tirade, yelling, and beating her fists on the door—the only part of the room not padded—until Gia heard a guard enter the room. The bass voice that spoke to Leilani told her she needed to calm down. Her daddy had paid for her to stay on the boat, but even his money wouldn't keep her there if she didn't control herself.

Stay on the boat?

But they said she'd be shipped off and banned! She'd been satisfied knowing that Leilani would be punished, but so much for that.

She fumed, hopping off her bed and pacing.

Gia's door opened next. "You're free to go."

"Did you let her go too?"

"Who?"

"The girl I was in a fight with?"

"I can't divulge information on other passengers."

But they did let her go. She heard them!

She knew better than to try to argue with them, though. The decision was probably made well above their paygrade, anyway. So Gia bit her tongue and followed the security guard through the crew area. When she exited onto the deck outside, Brett was waiting for her.

She ran into his arms, surprised at how relieved she was to see him.

Maybe it's just relief at being free.

No, it was also the reassurance of someone who had your back, no matter what.

The moment the security guard was gone, Brett and Gia walked along the deck, knowing that sooner or later, if Leilani was on board, she'd find them.

She did.

"You're lucky they broke us up when they did," Leilani snarled, her bodyguard Niall beside her.

"You're right. I am lucky. Because I didn't want to kill you, and you clearly don't know when to give up."

The woman really either couldn't admit that she was getting beaten, or she was delusional.

In any case, she turned to Brett. "You always were stupid," Leilani said, rolling her eyes. "Or maybe you just don't care if I get rid of your new girlfriend."

"That's enough," Gia snapped, stepping up.

"You're not ordering anyone around, and I'd thank you for not insulting my fated mate."

"Fated mate?" Something passed over Leilani's eyes. Was it jealousy? Or maybe that feeling when you deeply want something but you think it's out of reach for you. She didn't want Brett, but even seemingly evil women probably wanted to have love. To find the one they were meant to be with.

"Yeah, fated mate," Gia repeated. "Which means we're stronger together. Besides, you know I'm with the Cavallis. And I'm wondering, what would your daddy think if he knew you were risking peace over a wolf you specifically asked him to release from the Santibanez pack? Especially after he just bailed you out of jail and paid for you to be able to stay on the ship. What, he thinks you're just on some vacation and doesn't know you're chasing after your ex?"

"Don't you bring up my—"

"I can't *not*, Leilani," Gia snapped. "Because, like it or not, that's what this is. You take out one of Oren's employees. It's direct war. And I have a feeling your daddy is going to be pissed. You asked him to release Brett from your pack, and then you'd commit an act of war over him? I can't even imagine what repercussions that would have for *you*."

The wolf princess was clearly angry, but Gia had gone straight to the point.

Brett cleared his throat. "Sadly, Mr. Santibanez

isn't Leilani's biggest fan as it is. His kids like to boast about his power, but none actually do anything to contribute. I mean, an act like this could get someone disinherited and finally exiled from the pack. Mr. S. has done it for less." Brett shrugged as though the bomb he dropped was of no importance to him.

"Rude!" Leilani shouted.

"But true," Brett added.

"If not disowned, but probably at least banned from ever seeing Brett again," Gia added.

"You were a Santibanez wolf!" Leilani screamed. "He'll be glad I did something rather than allow you to move on with our enemies!"

Gia tapped her finger on her chin like she was deep in thought. "I mean, Mr. S. gave Brett special permission to leave the organization, so if Leilani backpedals now, it makes Mr. S.'s special dissolution of the marriage embarrassing to him, to his family. *That* would be worse, more shameful and embarrassing, to the family than for the ex to be with a rival family, don't you think?"

"Absolutely," Brett agreed. "As far as Mr. S. is concerned, once you're out, you're out. Being a *former Santibanez wolf* isn't a good thing in his eyes. It means I'm a cast-off."

"Stinky leftovers," Gia laughed.

"Right. I can go to a rival, and the shame is on the rival, not on Mr. S., especially considering all the time that's lapsed. It's not like I have any organization information anymore."

Leilani looked visibly sickened by the reasonable statements they were making. Gia could tell the woman hated being put in her place, but everything they said was true.

That, however, brought them to the next level of danger because when someone is cornered with no other options when they feel completely powerless, they'll lash out.

And if Leilani wanted to fight as shifters on the boat full of non-shifters, it would be worse than the fight broken up on the shifter island. Here, they risked exposing the shifter secret.

And fighting with teeth and claws would put innocents in danger.

Gia wracked her brain to try to think of how to diffuse the situation. The regular conflict resolution strategies she was trained in wouldn't go well. Leilani didn't want her pain validated by someone she viewed as her enemy.

"Hi, excuse me, but are you, Leilani Santibanez?" A timid male voice made all three turn.

"Who the hell is asking?" The moment Leilani locked eyes on the man, Gia saw something change within the woman.

Her face softened. Her eyes blinked. It was as though singing birds flew around the pair, and their irises turned heart-shaped while they stared at each other.

"I'm Parker Mirsky. I was told that if I flew here as fast as I could that I'd meet my fated mate." The relatively slim and short man spoke in a breathy voice like he couldn't believe his eyes. "You're so beautiful, though. I cannot believe that you're really her."

For a moment, Gia held her breath. Would Leilani accept the nerdy-looking man with smudged glasses and messy brown hair?

Leilani circled him like a fox scoping out the chicken coop. Though Gia and Brett still stood there, they were clearly forgotten.

A fashionable figure popped up at Gia's right. Esme let out a sigh. "I almost wasn't sure I was going to get this one done in time."

"You found Leilani's mate?" As if Gia really had to ask.

"And brought him here in a matter of days. Hours, really." Satisfied with what she saw, Esme crossed her arms in her designer blazer and gave Gia and Brett a wide smile.

"You're a bonafide miracle worker." Brett shook his head in amazement.

"Agreed," Gia added.

While Brett, Gia, and Esme watched Leilani and Parker walk off together—with the bodyguard Niall trailing behind—Gia couldn't help the fear she felt for the man. "Shouldn't we worry that she's going to do the same thing to him that she did to Brett?"

"No," Esme and Brett replied at the same time.

"You first." Esme motioned to Brett.

"He's a rabbit, for one," Brett explained. "The wolves would never let in a rabbit, like they did for me, a fellow gray wolf."

Esme added, "And he has his own empire. He lives in California. CEO of a tech giant. He wouldn't leave it for anything. Leilani will have to leave Colorado and start a new life as a socialite wife with him. I must say, her father will likely be relieved."

"Yeah, you did him a favor." Bret let out a little laugh and placed his arm around Gia. "You did us more than one favor. Thank you. For everything."

Gia echoed Brett's gratitude, but she still couldn't shake how much she hated watching Leilani walk off to her happily-ever-after.

"What's wrong, Gia?" Esme asked.

"It just seems a little unfair that she gets a happy ending after all the pain she caused."

Esme pursed her lips. "I don't help just anyone, you know. And while the main reason I found Parker was to help you two find *your* happy ending, sometimes finding your mate changes you. Having unconditional love and acceptance can sometimes mean a person stops feeling their life is out of control, making them stop needing to control others. Sometimes settling, and feeling happiness, is a way to dissolve the chaos and desperation that lives inside. And a level-headed mate like Parker has a good chance of being able to convince someone like Leilani to finally get the help they need."

"Therapy," Brett added.

Esme nodded in agreement.

"Maybe I just need some time to pass after what happened today to feel more charitable toward her," Gia muttered.

"Just keep in mind that there may be some point when she'll want to make things right," Esme warned. "And I think Brett already knows the importance of that, don't you?"

He nodded. "We're all here on this spinning ball together. Second chances, a chance to be a better person and use the rest of your years to make something positive for the world, that's our gift. And if her fated mate helps her become a better person, then good for her. Not that she'll ever be part of our lives, just that we can accept that people can better themselves."

"Couldn't agree more!" Esme clapped her hands together and took a deep breath. "Well, that's been a lot of excitement today, but a matchmaker's job is never done. I'm afraid I have to run!"

They bid Esme farewell and were finally left alone.

"Poor guy doesn't know what he's in for," Gia mused, still unable to stop worrying for the rabbit.

"Who knows, they're fated mates. They might just fit together perfectly." Brett pulled Gia into his arms and kissed the top of her head. "Maybe they'll bring out the best in each other."

Gia wasn't sure there was a best in Leilani, but she hoped there was something redeemable there for Parker Mirsky's sake.

If Esme thought there was, then maybe there was.

At least it set Gia and Brett free from Leilani's sights.

"Now, let's forget Leilani and Parker," Brett spoke softly in her ear, sending a chill down her spine. "All that is the past. It's all behind us. Now, looking forward, all I can see is you."

CHAPTER
ELEVEN

They had special reservations at the boat's most upscale restaurant that night. They found themselves tucked into a rounded booth, right by a window with a fantastic view of the sunset.

They took full advantage of the booth. It was the first dinner when they weren't seated across from each other, so Brett could place his arm around his shoulder and hold her close while they looked over the menu.

He was so happy to be there with her.

He didn't want to ruin it with an intense topic, but the time had come. "So, tomorrow we disembark."

Gia nodded. "And we fly home."

"To our individual homes."

"Right." Gia looked off to the side as though thinking and then looked back to him. "What are your thoughts on long-distance relationships?"

Those hadn't been the words he'd expected or hoped for, but it was better than the ones he'd dreaded. "I've never done one before, but for you, Gia, I'd be willing to try anything."

"Within reason." She reminded him of the healthy boundaries he'd set since being used and controlled by Leilani. "Honestly, I'm glad that you're not letting your past relationship with your ex stop you from the possibility of happiness with me."

He squeezed her shoulder and kissed her temple. "Part of recovery is forgiving myself and learning to trust myself. It's not easy. It can be scary, but the moment I saw you, I decided not to turn tail and run. The feelings between us are intense and overwhelming, but I'm facing it. Because you're worth it."

"Oh, Brett," Gia brushed her hand over his cheek. "*You're* worth it."

He couldn't help himself. He kissed her. Surely no one in that fancy romantic restaurant would mind?

When their lips parted, he took a deep breath. "The most terrifying part is embracing the hope of really having that chance of happiness you always dreamed of. That it might not be a trap like it was last time."

"It's opening your heart to the possibility of being broken again." Gia gave him a soft, beautiful smile that filled his heart with love. "But I can assure you, I would never want to hurt you."

"Gia, I'll do long-distance if you want, but all I know is that I don't want to live life without you. I know we have a lot of stuff to figure out, a lot of it within myself, learning to trust myself, learning that it's okay to trust others. Still, I know that meeting you has felt like entering a new level of life that I never knew existed. I won't live another day without thinking about you."

She nodded. "That's how I feel too. Yeah, it's complicated with the Oren vs. Mr. S. thing, but I think we can work it out. And I think it's worth it."

"How will we work it out, the Oren—"

"I've been thinking that maybe it's time for me to jump," Gia interrupted. "To start looking for a location for my bed and breakfast."

The moment she said it, a waiter approached the table. "Excuse me, ma'am, but I've been asked to deliver this for you."

"Oh, okay, thanks." Gia took the large envelope, and Brett saw the scrawled GW logo on it.

"It's from Esme." Gia opened it and withdrew several sheets of paper.

The first one had a handwritten letter from Esme.

Gia,

I hope you've had a wonderful cruise! I meant to discuss this with you earlier, but I've been busy dealing with one issue after another. Don't worry. I've managed to find solutions for everything!

In any event, here's what I wanted to discuss: Oren informed me that you're interested in running a bed and breakfast, and truth be told, I love staying in little places like that when I travel. Unfortunately, there isn't one near my favorite bakery outside of Denver.

So, I'd like to open one if I can find the right person to manage it. Would you be interested in a partnership? I found this little beauty that's been vacant for a while, but with a little work, I think it could really be something special!

Esme's contact information was beneath the note, and the following page was a map with a big circle on it.

"That's only about ten minutes from my bakery," Brett revealed.

The following page was a list of nearby points of interest, the top listing being Pastry Pack. There was also antique shopping, restaurants, entertainment, fishing, hiking, biking, parks, and a nearby river for rafting. "Everything you'd want near your B&B," Gia mused.

She flipped to the next page and gasped. "It's

beautiful! A late eighteen-hundreds two-story Victorian-style former bed and breakfast with seven bedrooms, five bathrooms, over four-thousand square feet."

She continued flipping the pages to look at other photos, describing them as she did. "Look! Tall ceilings, large rooms, beautiful floors!"

"The rooms are rather plain, aren't they?"

"That's the point! I can start from the ground up, designing the exact aesthetic I want. It looks like it needs a little restoration and TLC, but I can just see making it so cozy! Oh, and look, this one is meant to be a library and sitting room! Ah! *Gorgeous* bookcases!"

"You look so excited," Brett said, more interested in watching the joy on her face than the photos on the page.

"I am," she replied, thoroughly mesmerized by the papers in her hand.

"It fills my heart to see you that way. Gia, I would do anything to see you this happy for the rest of my life."

"Are you sure?" She finally looked up at him while holding the stack of papers to her heart. "Because it's going to be hard work getting this place up and running, and well... it will take a lot of my time."

"I will help in any way I can. I'll lift things, build things, paint things. And if you have crews for all that, then I'll make big batches of cookies and pastries to keep you all well-fed."

She threw her arms around his neck and kissed him. "You really mean that, don't you?"

"I do."

Her excitement was catching. They looked over the photos, again and again, pointing out little details until their meal arrived. They reluctantly returned the papers to the envelope, and they ate their dinner with visions of their future vivid in their minds.

Their future was bright.

Brighter than Brett ever thought possible.

He was certain about it in a way he'd never felt before. He'd always been an anxious person, worrying that he would have to struggle to hold on to what he had.

But with Gia? With the idea of her bed and break-fast coming to life with the help of Esme Baer? There was nothing but peace inside of him, knowing that it would all work out completely.

Was it scary to trust that kind of feeling? Yeah.

But Gia was worth it.

CHAPTER

TWELVE

The cruise seemed to go too quickly because they were disembarking before they knew it.

Brett waved to Bill when he saw him leaving, and Gia remarked that the redhead nearby was the friend she'd made, Ray.

Brett even caught sight of Leilani and her mate.

Good luck to them, Brett thought.

He had better things to concern himself with.

Brett walked with Gia to the shuttle stop. They were leaving from different airports, so when it was time to split, they turned to look at each other.

"So, now what?"

"I guess I'll work with Esme on moving forward with the bed and breakfast. It's just a matter of what I'm going to do while everything gets moved into place"— She fiddled with the handle on her suitcase, staring intently at it while she spoke.—"I could keep working for Oren, or"—She finally looked up, locking eyes with him.—"I could see about getting a job closer to the location."

Closer to him, Brett thought. "Yeah, I like that idea. The you being closer part."

He hugged her and planted a kiss on her lips. The plane ride and their time apart from her would be torture.

"Question. Does the person who runs the bed and breakfast usually live there?"

"Yeah, usually." Gia nodded.

"So"—Brett breathed, thinking about how the place that would be her business could possibly be much more personal for the two of them, too.—"it's not just designing your business, but your home too?"

She understood what he was saying. "Yes. Designing *our* home."

Brett's phone began to chime. Text messages were finally coming back in since he'd had no service while they were out to sea.

"Everything okay?" Gia peered at him curiously while he pulled the device out to check the messages.

"Bunch of stuff from my brother, hang on. I'm going to call him."

Thatcher answered with a tone of excitement. "When are you going to be back? I need you to get here and run the shop for a bit. I have to leave town."

"What? For how long?" Brett asked.

"I don't know. I'm not sure."

"Are you in some kind of trouble?" Brett's heart stopped for a moment, fearing the worst.

"No, nothing like that!" Thatcher reassured him. "I promise, I'm fine. It's actually a good thing. I'm in a baking contest! Now, I know that we always said we'd do one together, one of those shows with partners, but this one came up and…"

"It's fine," Brett laughed, looking at Gia. "I have plenty to keep me distracted. Go out to Hollywood or wherever it is, and show the world what the Cowans Bakery is all about."

Thatcher sighed, clearly relieved. "I just need to know you'll be back soon to run things."

"No problem, bro. I'll be home in a few hours."

He hung up the phone and turned back to Gia. "Looks like my brother has to go out of town for a bit, so I happen to be in need of some help at the bakery. You interested?"

Her face lit up at the idea. "Only if you promise to make those honey cookies you mentioned."

"Anything for you."

The End.

Stay tuned for Thatcher's story! We'll see another familiar Idlewyld face there, too. Can you guess who?

ALSO BY RENEE HEWETT

FURRY UNITED COALITION NEWBIE ACADEMY

Goose and the Ocelot

Moose and the Narwhal

Zeus and the Raptor

THE NIGHTSHADE GUILD

Sunny Mage

Magic Clouded

Illuminating Time

CRIMSON MOON HIDEAWAY

Chimera's Edge

Harpy's Escape

Flame and Mist

About the Author

Renee Hewett writes paranormal romance. Before becoming a full-time writer she worked in marketing, web writing, and editing. She's volunteered for at many events, such as C4 Comic Con, Can-Con, and Romancing the Capital.

ReneeHewett.com
Facebook reader group
Sign up for Renee's Newsletter